Don't Laugh, Joe!

Keiko Kasza

G. P. Putnam's Sons   New York

For Yoshiyuki, Chiaki, and Ami

Library of Congress Cataloging-in-Publication Data
Kasza, Keiko. Don't laugh, Joe!/Keiko Kasza. p. cm.
Summary: Mother Possum is in despair because her son cannot learn
to play dead without laughing.
[1. Opossums--Fiction. 2. Laughter--Fiction. 3. Mothers and sons--Fiction.] I. Title.
PZ7.K15645Do 1997 [E]--dc20 95-25534 CIP AC
ISBN 0-399-23036-X

1 3 5 7 9 10 8 6 4 2
First Impression

Mother Possum dearly loved her little son Joe, but he was always giggling. Lately his giggling made her worry. Mother Possum was about to teach Joe the most important lesson a possum can learn.

"Joe," said Mother Possum, "you must learn how to play dead."

"Why?" asked Joe.

"Because we possums escape our enemies by playing dead," Mother Possum explained. "When you learn this trick, Joe, I'll bake you the possums' favorite dessert—a bug pie!"

They started to practice.

"No giggling, Joe," Mother Possum warned.

"No problem, Mom," Joe answered.

Joe played dead, and his mother sniffed his fur like a hungry fox.

Sniff, sniff, sniff.

Joe laughed so hard that his stomach hurt. "Can I have my pie now?" he asked.

"No way, Joe," Mother Possum scolded. "Dead possums don't laugh!"

Joe practiced playing dead again. This time his mother poked him like a nasty coyote.

Poke, poke, poke.

Joe laughed so hard that he screamed for her to stop. "Can I have my pie now?" he asked.

"No way, Joe," Mother Possum scolded. "Dead possums don't scream!"

Joe practiced playing dead once more.
This time his mother shook him like a
scary wildcat.

Shake, shake, shake.

Joe laughed so hard that he wiggled
loose and fell on the floor.

"How about some bug pie, Mom?" he
asked.

"No way, Joe," Mother Possum scolded.
"Dead possums don't wiggle!"

Joe's mother was worried about his laughing, but his friends loved it. They liked to watch Joe play dead because he made them laugh, too.

"But, Joe," Mother Possum said, sighing, "what will you do when real danger comes?"

One day, Mother Possum took Joe outside to practice. "This time," she said, "I'll be a grumpy old bear. When I growl at you, you play dead. Okay, Joe?"

"Nothing to it, Mom," Joe said.

But just as Mother Possum was about to growl ...

... a real grumpy old bear came out of the woods. He let out the fiercest growl Joe had ever heard. Joe and his mother immediately fell to the ground to play dead.

The grumpy old bear sniffed Joe's fur.
Sniff, sniff, sniff.

The grumpy old bear poked Joe's tummy.
Poke, poke, poke.

Finally, the grumpy old bear shook Joe up and down.
Shake, shake, shake.

Joe didn't laugh. Joe didn't scream. Joe didn't wiggle.
For the first time, he played dead perfectly. Mother
Possum was very proud of him. But the grumpy old
bear wouldn't go away. He sat and sat and sat.

Suddenly, the bear started to cry big tears.
"This is terrible," he moaned. "I'm always so
grumpy. I thought that if anyone could make
me laugh, it would be little Joe the possum.
But when I find him, poor Joe drops dead
before my eyes! Oh, this is awful!"

When he heard the bear's story, Joe was relieved. He even began to feel sorry for the sobbing bear. "Hey, Mr. Bear," he called, "I'm not dead. I was just playing dead."

The bear was so surprised he almost jumped out of his fur. "Playing dead?" he cried. "Boy, you're good at that! Oh, please, Joe," he begged, "teach me how to laugh."

"It's easy," said Joe. "Lots of things are funny, Mr. Bear. What happened just now is funny," and he started to giggle. Soon his laughter spread to everyone around him, even to the grumpy old bear.

Before long, the animals were laughing
so hard that the whole forest shook.

"Oh, Joe," the bear howled, "thank
you for teaching me to laugh."

"Thank you, Mr. Bear," Joe answered,
"for teaching me how to play dead."

"Now can I have my pie?" Joe asked his mother.

"Absolutely," Mother Possum answered. "Everyone, please come and join us for some delicious bug pie."

"With grasshoppers!" Joe shouted gleefully. "And beetles and yummy cockroaches, too!"

The other animals suddenly stopped their giggling.
"Bug pie??? Cockroaches!!!" One by one, they fell to
the ground …

... and played dead.

Ink + pencil
scribbles
3-4-11